Riley Royce And

Illustrated by Alexandria Green

WHO STOLE MY BOW?

Copyright © 2024 by Riley Royce Anderson

All rights reserved. No part of this book may be reproduced or transmitted in any form or by any means, electronic or mechanical, including photocopying, recording, or any information storage and retrieval system, without permission in writing from the author.

ISBN: 978-1-6653-0925-7

∞ This paper meets the requirements of ANSI/NISO Z39.48-1992 (Permanence of Paper)

Cover and Interior Art by Alexandria Green

081924

I dedicate this book to:
my Mom Toshia,
my Dad Roy,
My big brother in heaven Roosevelt Anderson III aka Tres'
My big sister Rosalind Nate' Anderson
my baby brother Roosevelt IV "RJ"
my nephews Machi and Jehlani
my dog Snoop
and my big cousin RaRa for always making me read and my Nana for making me sweet.
I love you all.

And…
My favorite hair stylists, Nichole Askew and Nita Freeman aka V.
Thanks for always keeping my hair cute with my favorite bows!! Love you both!

Mom comes in to tuck me in.
I love my mom.

I grab my favorite pillow to go to sleep with.

But I have to say my prayers first.

"Good night family!" I shout one last time.

Who stole my bow?

But no one knows...

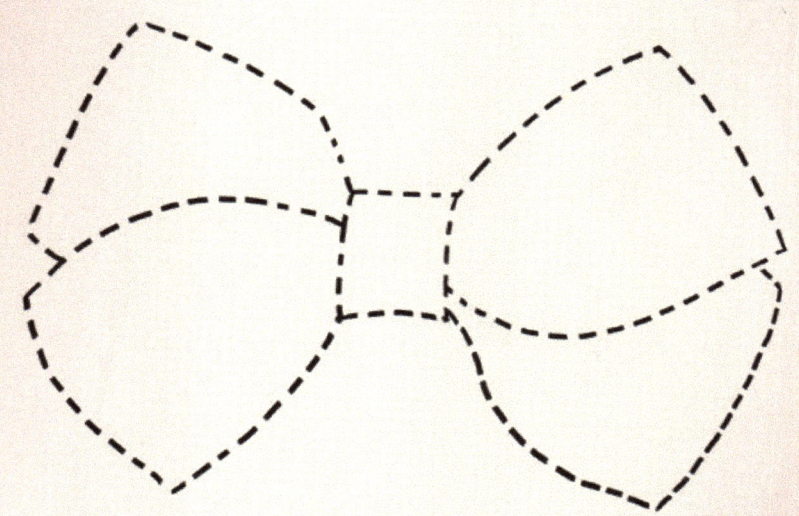

WHO...stole...*my*...bow?

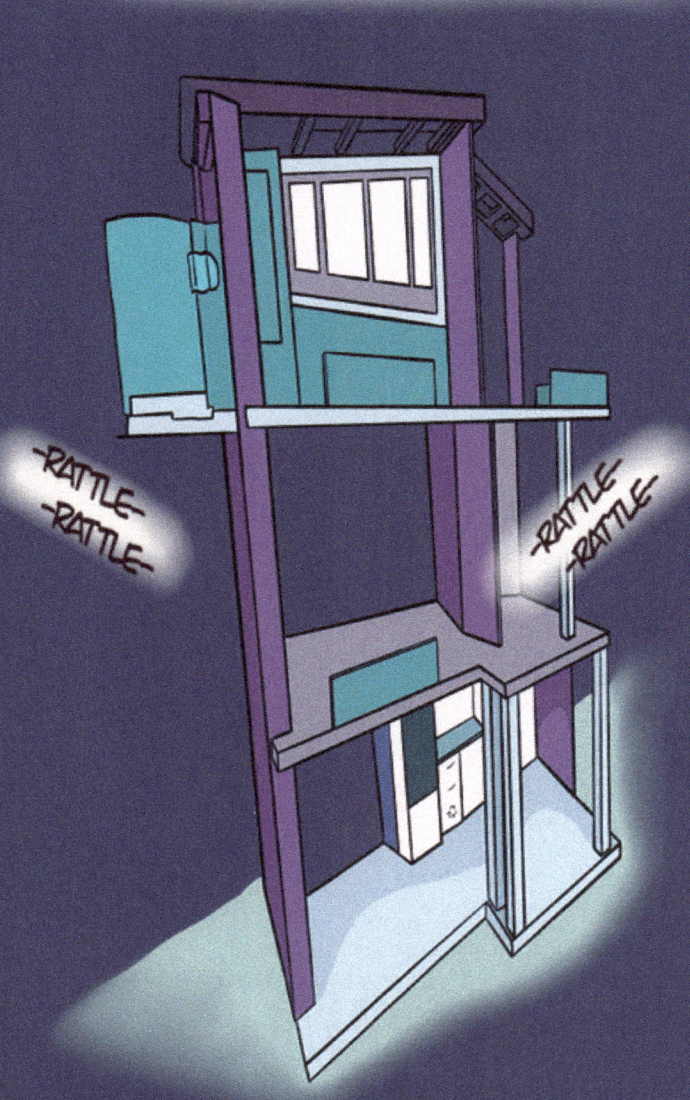

It's coming from my doll house.

What could it be?

Is it you?

Is it me?

It's big!

No, it's small!

It's my doll?!

My doll stole my bow!

The End!

My name is Riley Royce Anderson and I'm a fun, loving, nine-year-old in the 4th grade. I attend a great elementary school in Stockbridge, GA.

I love reading, writing, swimming, skating, cooking, acting and playing with my friends.